# Read and Think Book 2

# Hip, Kit, Ping, and Ig

### Written by:
C. D. Buchanan, Jim Hunter, and Michele Navarrete

### Art by:
Frank Hill and Carol Andrews Moore

07-063202-2

6 7 8 9 0 VHVH 8 3 2 1

WEBSTER DIVISION, McGRAW-HILL BOOK COMPANY
St. Louis · New York · San Francisco · Dallas · Toronto · London · Sydney

Hip has a
kitchen band.

Hap is in Hip's band.
Is that a bat in Hap's hand?

Yes. Hap hits a pan.
Bang! Bang! Bang!

Is that Hap?
Can Hap tap?

No. It is Fan Fan.
Fan Fan taps on a tin can.

Hap's cat
rings on the mat.

7

PAT! BANG! PAT! BANG

TAP! TAP! TAP!

Is that Hap?
And his pan?

BANG!
BANG!

No, Hap's bang is
a big BANG BANG!

It is Fan Fan's fish
in a tin dish.
The fish's fin
pats the tin.

11

TAP! TAP!

Fan Fan taps.

PAT! BANG!
PAT! BANG!

The fish pats.

BANG! BANG!

Hap bangs.

RING! DING!

DING! RING!

The cat rings.

My band is best!

Hip sings.

# SAD, SAD KIT

Kit is digging in the sand.

Kit is scratching and scratching.

Is Sam in the kitchen?  Is Ann in?

No. Kit is a sad, sad kitten.

Can I sit in this can?

No, no, no.

Kit! Kit!
Is that Ann?

Yes it is, yes it is!

Ann has the dripping kitten.

Kit licks Ann's chin.

# PING AND HIS PINS

**Ping is a pin man.**

Pins, pins, pins!

Ping has pink pins.

Ping has red pins.

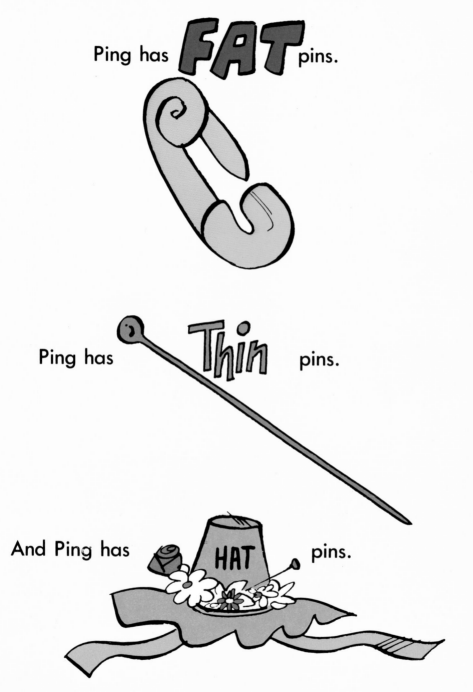

Ping has **FAT** pins.

Ping has **Thin** pins.

And Ping has **HAT** pins.

Has Ping a tan pin?

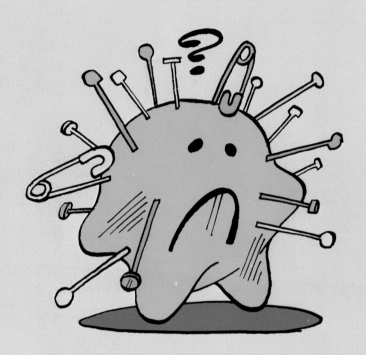

No, Ping has
pink pins and
red pins.

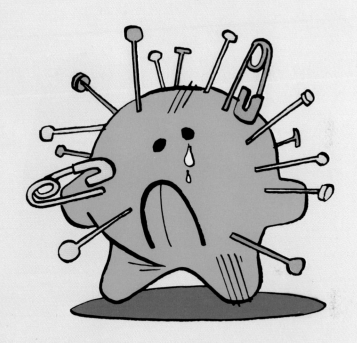

Ping, the pin man,
is sad. No tan
pins!

Scratch, the chicken,
stands on the mat.

Scratch has a map.

The pin man
ran and ran,
sack in hand,
to the sand.

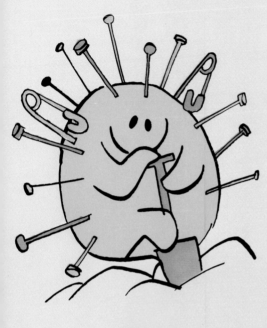

Dig!
Dig!

Scratch!
Scratch!

Pins,

pins,

pins,

pins!

The tan pin is best,
Ping sings!

A tan pin!
A tan pin!
Ping has a tan pin!

# THE HAT IN THE SAND

Sam is digging in the sand.

Ann is sitting in the sand.
Ann has mints in a bag.

Sam has a tan hat on.

Ann has a pink hat on.

Nip has Sam's tan hat.

Sam and Ann ran to catch Nip.

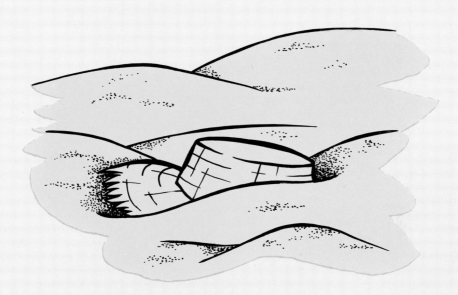

Nip hid Sam's hat in the sand.

Ann pats Len's hand.

Sam has the tan hat back.

Sam, Ann, and Len
sit on the sand and nap.
The hat is on Len's lap.

And Nip?
Nip has Ann's bag of mints!

# IG, THE RAG PIG

This is Ig,
the rag pig.

And this patch and Ken's pants match!

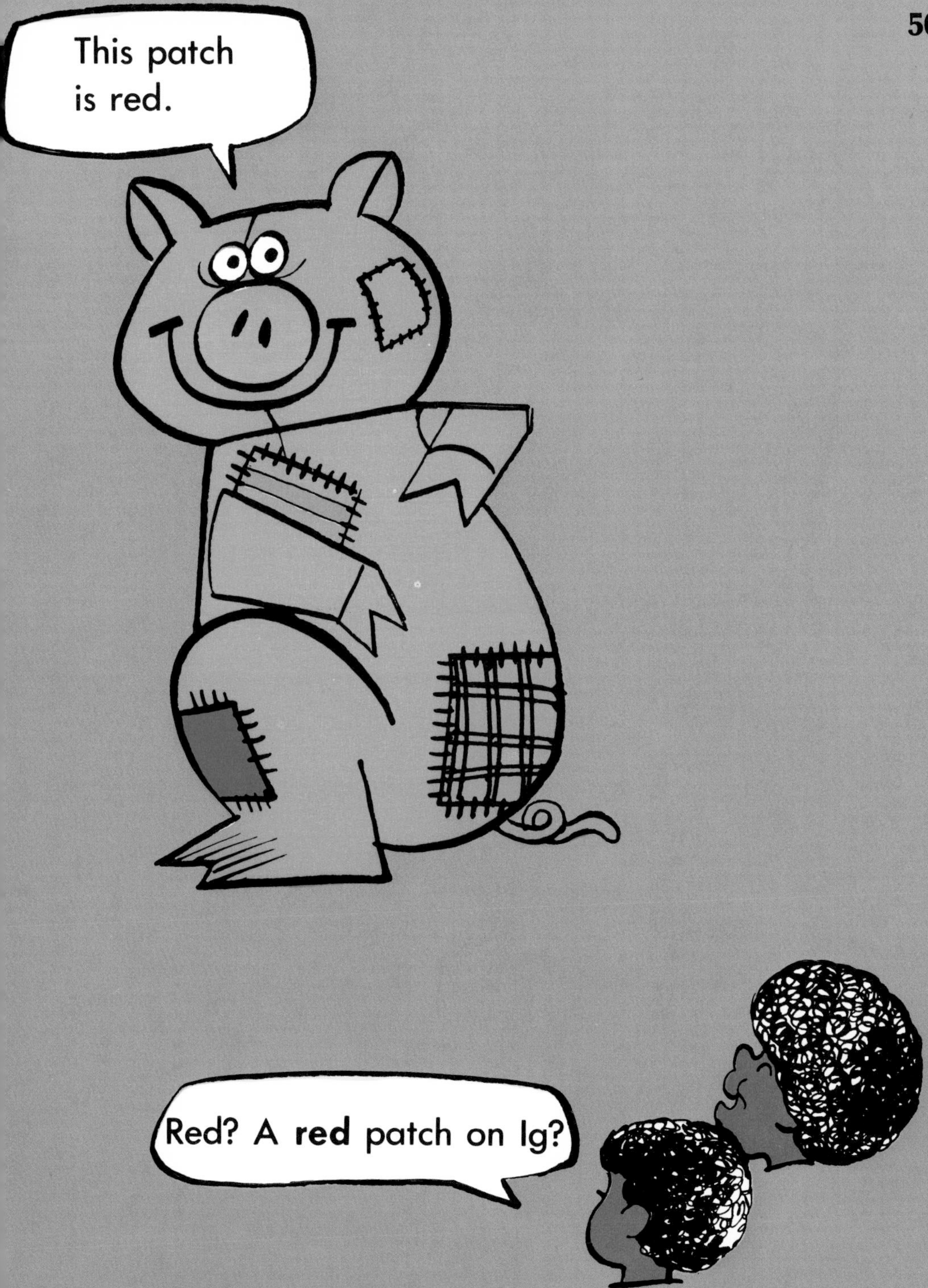
This patch
is red.
Red? A **red** patch on Ig?

Is the pink and tan patch
on the mat?

No, it is on Ig's back.

Ig and Pam nap!

That Ig!